Curious George®
Colors Eggs

Adaptation by Kate O'Sullivan
Based on the TV series teleplay
written by Michael Maurer

SCHOLASTIC INC.

ISBN 978-0-545-85463-4

Curious George television series merchandise © 2011 Universal Studios. Curious George and
related characters, created by Margret and H. A. Rey, are copyrighted and registered by
Houghton Mifflin Harcourt Publishing Company and used under license.
Licensed by Universal Studios Licensing LLC. All rights reserved. Published by Scholastic Inc.,
557 Broadway, New York, NY 10012, by arrangement with Houghton Mifflin Harcourt Publishing Company.
The PBS KIDS logo is a registered trademark of PBS and is used with permission. Green Light Readers®
and its logo are trademarks of HMH Publishers LLC, registered in the United States and other countries.
All rights reserved. LEXILE® is a registered trademark of MetaMetrics, Inc. SCHOLASTIC and associated
logos are trademarks and/or registered trademarks of Scholastic Inc.

12 11 10 9 8   18 19 20/0

Printed in the U.S.A.   40

First Scholastic printing, March 2015

Design by Afsoon Razavi

AGES	GRADES	GUIDED READING LEVEL	READING RECOVERY LEVEL	LEXILE ® LEVEL
5-7	1-2	I	15-16	330L

George was excited.
He was spending the day with
Betsy and Steve.

They were going to dye eggs!
There would be an egg hunt later.
The man with the yellow hat gave
George an apron.
"I am leaving for my bird-watching
trip with Chef Pisghetti. Please try to
stay clean while I am gone," he said.

Steve showed George three pots of dye. One was red. One was blue. And one was yellow.
"These are called primary colors," Steve said.
"You can make every color in the rainbow. Just mix them in different ways."

George was very curious.

Steve dipped an egg in the yellow dye.

Then Steve
dipped the egg
in the blue dye.
The egg turned green!

George had an idea.

He dipped a
banana in blue dye.
Then he dipped it in the red dye.
George made the banana turn
purple!

Charkie was curious, too.
She wanted to see the purple
banana up close.

She chased after George.
As they ran, Charkie bumped the
tables. One started to roll.

It knocked down a mop.
The mop bumped a shelf.
And the cake on the shelf started to fall!

George jumped, losing his apron.
He saved the cake!
But it was very heavy.
His feet started to slip . . .

"Oh, no, George!" Steve cried.
He and Betsy grabbed the cake.
But George fell into the pot! "You were
supposed to stay clean," said Betsy.

But George had another idea.
If red and blue made purple,
could he mix the right colors to make
brown?

George jumped into the red dye.
But yellow and red made orange,
not brown.

George and his
friends heard footsteps in the hall.
"Quick—hide!" Steve said.
George jumped into the sink.

"How was the egg dyeing?" the
man with the yellow hat asked.
"And where's George?" asked
Chef Pisghetti.

George popped up from the sink. "Thanks for staying clean," said his friend. George had picked the perfect hiding place.

Colors, Colors, Everywhere!

Circle all of the objects in primary colors (red, yellow, blue).